Today Is Thanksgiving!

by P. K. Hallinan

ideals children's books.
Nashville, Tennessee

ISBN 0-8249-5325-8 (case)
ISBN 0-8249-5326-6 (paper)

Published by Ideals Children's Books
An imprint of Ideals Publications
A division of Guideposts
535 Metroplex Drive, Suite 250
Nashville, Tennessee 37211
www.idealspublications.com

Copyright © 1993 by P. K. Hallinan

All rights reserved. No part of this publication may be reproduced or transmitted in any form or by any means, electronic or mechanical, including photocopy, recording, or any information storage and retrieval system, without permission in writing from the publisher.

Printed and bound in Mexico.

Library of Congress CIP data on file.

For Jeanne, with thanks for a lifetime

Other Books by P. K. Hallinan

A Rainbow of Friends

For the Love of Our Earth

Heartprints

How Do I Love You?

I'm Thankful Each Day!

Just Open a Book

Let's Learn All We Can!

My Dentist, My Friend

My Doctor, My Friend

My First Day of School

My Teacher's My Friend

That's What a Friend Is

Today Is Christmas!

Today Is Easter!

Today Is Halloween!

Today Is Valentine's Day!

Today Is Your Birthday!

We're Very Good Friends, My Brother and I

We're Very Good Friends, My Father and I

We're Very Good Friends, My Grandma and I

We're Very Good Friends, My Grandpa and I

We're Very Good Friends, My Mother and I

We're Very Good Friends, My Sister and I

When I Grow Up

10 8 6 4 2 1 3 5 7 9

Today is Thanksgiving,
and an icicle breeze
nips at your window
and whips up the leaves.

Ah, what a morning!
The cold autumn haze
brings visions of Pilgrims
and Indians . . . and maize!

So wrap in a blanket
and don your warm socks
and pretend you're descending
on old Plymouth rock.

And with football in tow,
downstairs you go.

Already the kitchen's
beginning to swell
with all the aromas
you know oh-so-well!

The scent of potatoes
rides lightly on air.
The fragrance of turkey
encircles your hair.

And the pie's slowly baking—
it's apple, you're guessing—
while celery stalks boil
to help make the dressing.

And you gladly pitch in,
rolling dough nice and thin.

Then it's off to the den,
where the TV is tuned
to a colorful parade,
full of floats and balloons!

And you watch for awhile,
but soon it's all done,
so you roll out the door
for a stroll in the sun.

And the chilly air tweaks
your nose and your cheeks.

Now here come your friends
racing onto the scene!
They're ready for football
in their jerseys and jeans!

So you quickly choose sides
and mark off the goals,
using jackets and earmuffs
and telephone poles.

Then with one mighty kick
the game starts to click.

And oh, what a game!
So many trick plays!
You sneak to the mailbox,
then streak the wrong way!

But then a long pass
over driveway and grass
is caught near the earmuffs—
a touchdown at last!

And everyone sighs
as you end in a tie.

Later, back home
you quickly get dressed
and shine like a diamond
to impress all your guests.

And here they are now!
It's the whole family clan!
Why, it's dear Auntie Pansy
and big Uncle Stan!

And everyone's bearing
some food for the sharing.

Soon there are roomfuls
of nephews and nieces.
The cat's on the table—
the dog's got the sneezes.

And Uncle Tobias
is asleep in the chair,
while Petey the parakeet
creeps in his hair.

And the whole house resounds
with hilarious sounds.

The time has arrived
for the meal to begin,
so you dash to your chair
with a flair and a grin.

And the hot giblet gravy
brings loud "oohs" and "ahs,"
but the sight of the turkey
draws a round of applause.

Then all heads are lowered,
as you join in a prayer,
giving thanks for your blessings
and the gifts waiting there.

And with grace at an end,
you whisper, "Amen."

The meal is a wonder,
a cranberry dream.
There's a crisp garden salad
and fruit in whipped cream.

And the portions keep coming—
the rolls and the yams—
till your tummy's so full
it's too crammed to expand.

But you let out a sigh
and make room for pie.

The evening soon fades
into games and charades,
and the clan drifts away
like a tired parade.

Then, alas, it's all over,
the laughter and fun,
for now Auntie Pansy
has hugged everyone.

So you head up to bed,
then stand in your room,
gazing out of the window
at the gold harvest moon.

And the last thing you do
is smile and say . . .

"Thank you for Thanksgiving!
What a wonderful day!"